# The Science of Primates

**LIVING SCIENCE**

Samantha Paterson

Weigl Publishers Inc.

**Published by Weigl Publishers Inc.**
123 South Broad Street, Box 227
Mankato, MN 56002
USA

Library of Congress Cataloging-in-Publication Data available upon request from the publisher.
Fax (507) 388-2746 for the attention of the Publishing Records Department.

ISBN 1-930954-36-0

**Project Co-ordinator:** Jared Keen
**Series Editor:** Celeste Peters
**Copy Editor:** Heather Kissock
**Design:** Warren Clark
**Cover Design:** Terry Paulhus
**Layout:** Lucinda Cage

Photograph Credits:
Corel Corporation: cover (background), pages 4 right, 5, 9, 10 left, 10 right, 11, 12 left, 13, 14 right, 15 top, 17 left, 20, 21 top center, 21 top right, 21 bottom left, 23 left, 30 left; Digital Vision: page 27; Gorilla Foundation/Koko.org: page 29 (Dr. Ronald Cohn); Martha Jones: page 22; J. D. Paterson: pages 4 left, 16 right, 17 right, 19, 24, 25 bottom; Tom Stack & Associates: pages 6 right (Gary Milburn), 7 top center (Inga Spence), 7 left (W. Perry Conway), 8 bottom right (Dominique Braud), 10 center left (Gary Milburn), 25 top (Tom & Therisa Stack); Monique St. Croix: pages 6 left, 12 right, 16 left, 23 right, 26; Visuals Unlimited: cover (center) (Inga Spence), pages 7 right (Ken Lucas), 8 top right (Fritz Polking), 8 left (Fritz Polking), 10 center right (Ken Lucas), 14 left (Gerald & Buff Corsi), 15 bottom (Inga Spence), 18 (Joe McDonald), 21 top left (Joe McDonald), 21 bottom right (John D. Cunningham), 28 (Ken Lucas), 30 right (Albert J. Copley), 31 left (Albert J. Copley), 31 right (Joe McDonald).

Printed in the United States of America
1 2 3 4 5 6 7 8 9 05 04 03 02 01

LIVING SCIENCE

# Contents

AEB - 7536

# What Do You Know about Primates?

Have you ever seen a chimpanzee at the zoo? Have you ever watched a television program showing a lemur leaping from tree to tree? Both big chimpanzees and little lemurs belong to a group of animals called primates. Human beings are also primates.

A primate is a type of **mammal**. Like all mammals, primates have fur or hair on their bodies. They are warm-blooded, and the young drink milk from their mothers. Human bodies have more in common with the bodies of chimpanzees and lemurs than with the bodies of other types of mammals.

Primates come in many shapes and sizes.

Human beings are like nonhuman primates in other ways, too, but they are also very different. For example, humans have the largest brain of any living primate. No other primate can talk the same way a human does, either.

Humans have always shared a special bond with other primates. People who lived a long time ago often told stories and painted pictures of what nonhuman primates looked like. Today, many people still like to watch nonhuman primates live and play.

## Activity

### Draw a Primate

Think of a primate. What kind of creature do you see in your mind? Draw a picture of that creature. Now compare it with the pictures of primates found in this book.

Ancient Egyptians believed that Hamadryas baboons were related to one of their gods. Sometimes they buried baboon mummies with human mummies.

# Primate Features

Primates have features that make them different from other mammals. These particular features help primates survive in the places they live.

## Primate Hands

**can grasp branches and catch insects in midair.** With hands that each have four bending fingers and a moving thumb, primates can grip objects tightly. Soft pads on their fingers also give them a fine sense of touch.

## Primate Eyes

**can tell when food is ripe and judge how far away the food is.** Most primates see things in full color. Both eyes can focus on a single object, which gives primates **three-dimensional vision**.

## Upright Posture and Strong Legs help primates stand tall.

All primates can stand straight up on their back legs. Being able to stand helps primates spot **predators** and other dangers.

## Primate Teeth can chew both meat and plants.

With teeth that can bite and chew, primates can eat vegetables, fruits, and even other animals.

## A Collarbone helps primates swing freely.

This bone is at the base of a primate's neck. It works with the shoulder blades to allow primates to move their arms in all directions.

## Puzzler

Sloths are furry animals. Their feet have two or three toes with hooklike claws, and they like to hang upside down in trees. Is a sloth a primate?

Answer: No. Although sloths live in trees, just as many primates do, they are not primates. They do not have thumbs or fingers. Sloths belong to a different group of mammals. They have more in common with anteaters than with primates.

# Life Cycles

The life cycle of a primate is much like the life cycle of any other mammal. Before it is born, a primate baby grows inside its mother's body. This growing time lasts for many months.

newborn

juvenile

A Japanese macaque baby grows inside its mother for six months. After it is born, the baby grows into a **juvenile**, then an adult. An adult macaque can have babies of its own.

adult

The length of time a baby spends growing inside its mother is less for smaller primates than it is for larger primates. The babies of other kinds of mammals often spend much less time inside their mothers.

Primates have longer childhoods than many other mammals do, too. They often stay close to their mothers until they become adults. By that time, they can find their own food and take care of themselves.

## Activity

### Time to Grow

Have a teacher or a parent help you find out how long each of these animals spends inside its mother's body before it is born.

- a cat
- a dog
- an elephant
- a horse
- a howler monkey
- a human being

A young grizzly bear leaves its mother after two years. A male chimpanzee stays with its mother for eight or nine years.

# Primate Types

There are more than 200 different kinds of primates. Scientists put primates into groups called families. Grouping primates makes studying them easier.

## Primate Families

| Lemurs | Tarsiers | Lorises | Bush Babies |
|---|---|---|---|
| • live in trees or on the ground<br><br>• mark a territory with a smell<br><br>• are found only on Madagascar and smaller islands nearby | • are predators<br><br>• have very large eyes<br><br>• can turn their heads to see behind them | • creep up trees, rarely leap<br><br>• have a single long claw on each hind foot<br><br>• live alone or in small groups | • can leap 15 feet (4.5 meters) between trees<br><br>• can turn ears toward sounds<br><br>• hop like kangaroos |

## Examples

| | | | |
|---|---|---|---|
| aye-aye, ring-tailed lemur, sifaka | Dian's tarsier, pygmy tarsier, spectral tarsier | potto, slender loris, slow loris | dwarf galago, needle-clawed bush baby |

## Puzzler

Which primate is the largest? Which is the smallest?

Answer:
The largest primate alive today is the lowland gorilla. It can weigh up to 550 pounds (250 kilograms). The smallest primate is the pygmy mouse lemur. It weighs only 1 ounce (30 grams)!

| Old World Monkeys | New World Monkeys | Lesser Apes | Apes |
|---|---|---|---|
| • cannot grasp objects with tail | • can grasp objects with tail | • swing through trees | • have no tail |
| • have thirty-two teeth | • have thirty-six teeth | • have very long arms | • most build nests for beds |
| • have narrow noses | • have wide, round noses | • use arms for balance | • use tools to dig and to grind food |

| baboon, mandrill, mangabey, langur | capuchin, howler monkey, spider monkey, tamarin | gibbon, siamang | chimpanzee, gorilla, orangutan |

# All Thumbs

One very special feature of a primate is its thumbs. Compare the paw of a dog or the hoof of a horse to the hand of a primate. Can a dog or a horse use its paws or its hooves the same way a primate can use its hands? Why are the thumbs of primates so important?

Without thumbs, humans might not be able to draw, carve, or build things. Having thumbs and a large brain helps people do things other animals cannot do.

Like primates, koalas have thumbs. Koalas are not primates, though. They are **marsupials.**

A gibbon's thumbs allow it to grip branches and hold food.

Nonhuman primates do not build cities or make fancy carvings, but they do use their thumbs to climb and to grasp tools. Smaller primates escape from predators by climbing trees. They also climb to reach food growing high in the treetops. Larger primates use tools to find food, too. A chimpanzee, for example, will sometimes push a twig into a termite mound. Then it can eat the termites that crawl onto the twig.

## Activity

### Thumbs Up!

Fold your thumb into the palm of your hand. Now pick up a crayon using only your fingers. Draw a circle. Pick up the crayon again, using both your thumb and your fingers. Draw another circle. Is it easier to hold on to objects when you use your thumb?

A spider monkey uses its hands, feet, and tail to grab onto branches as it swings through the trees.

# Primate Homes

The place where an animal lives is called its habitat. Humans can live just about anywhere on Earth. They build shelters and grow their own food. Most nonhuman primates live in the forests or grasslands of Africa, Asia, Central America, and South America. Some make their homes in tall trees. Others live on the ground.

Several types of nonhuman primates live in South America's Amazon rain forest. A rain forest is moist and warm, so plants grow there all year long. With so much food to offer, the rain forest is home to many primates. Scientists do not even know the exact number. They keep finding more!

Mountain gorillas live in cool rain forests that are found on tall mountains.

Golden lion tamarins live in the warm rain forests of Brazil.

Only a small number of nonhuman primates live in woodland forests and grasslands. These places get less rainfall than a rain forest does, so fewer kinds of plants grow there. Food is harder to find. During dry times, food can be very scarce.

Vervet monkeys live in the woodlands south of the Sahara Desert in Africa.

People often chop down the forests in which primates live. Some primates then move closer to farms and cities to find food. African baboons kill chickens and eat the grain that grows on farms.

**Some langurs make their homes in the cities of India, where they are often seen begging for food.**

## Puzzler

Imagine a primate with long arms and a grasping tail. Would it live on the ground or in a tall tree?

Answer: This primate probably lives in a tree. Long arms and a grasping tail help a primate move through high branches. Primates that live on the ground do not need tails. Apes do not even have tails.

# Team Players

**M**ost primates live in groups. Some live in a small family group. Family members include a mother, a father, and their young. Other primates live in a larger group called a troop. Some troops have hundreds of members.

Living in a group makes it easier to raise young. Some female primates even care for each other's babies. Group members keep an eye out for predators and help protect each other from harm. Most primate troops claim a territory to live in, and they defend their territory against other troops.

A troop of squirrel monkeys can have up to 300 members.

A troop of baboons usually has 30 to 40 members.

Most primate troops have leaders. The leaders help troop members work together. Most often, the leaders are the older members of the group. They show younger members how to behave around each other. They also use their power to stop fights between group members.

Primates do not always spend their entire lives in just one troop. Some juveniles leave their troops to find mates in other groups. Sometimes troops split into smaller groups when food is hard to find.

Female Japanese macaques choose their troops' male leaders.

Male silverback gorillas are the leaders of their troops.

## Puzzler

A troop defends its territory from other animals of its own kind. Why?

Answer:
When a troop has found good food, it often does not want to share it with another troop. A troop does not want to share its members either. When members leave to join another group, they take away strength from the troop.

# Special Effects

**P**rimates often have **distinctive** features. Some have colorful faces or long noses. Others have extraordinary hair growth. These features make them stand out among other primates. Although their features might look unusual to humans, they often help the primates defend themselves or find mates.

The male proboscis monkey of Borneo has a very long nose. It keeps growing even after the monkey has become an adult. *Proboscis* means "nose."

Primates with large or colorful features are usually males. Many males use their distinctive features to attract females. Some primates have mustaches or beards, which make it easier to tell the males from the females. Other features help primates appear larger than they really are to scare away predators that might harm members of the troop.

Orangutans have large pads on the sides of their faces. These pads make the animal look bigger than it actually is.

# Web of Life

**D**o monkeys eat bananas? Some do, but primates also like to eat other foods. Primates that eat mostly fruit are called **frugivores**. Spider monkeys and squirrel monkeys are frugivores, but they eat insects or plant shoots, too.

Most primates are **omnivores**. They eat ants, termites, and other insects along with fruits and leaves. Some primates also eat eggs and small animals, if they can find them.

Chimpanzees and tarsiers are **carnivores**. They are among the few primates that eat meat. Tarsiers hunt insects, snails, and lizards. Chimpanzees will sometimes eat small animals, such as wild pigs and monkeys.

Baboons travel up to 12 miles (19 kilometers) a day looking for food.

Like all animals, primates are part of a food chain. All primates eat other living things to gain energy. Energy passes from the plant or animal that is eaten to the animal that eats it.

A fig tree uses energy from the Sun to grow fruit. Primates, such as gibbons, eat the figs that grow on these trees. Larger animals, such as leopards, eat the gibbons.

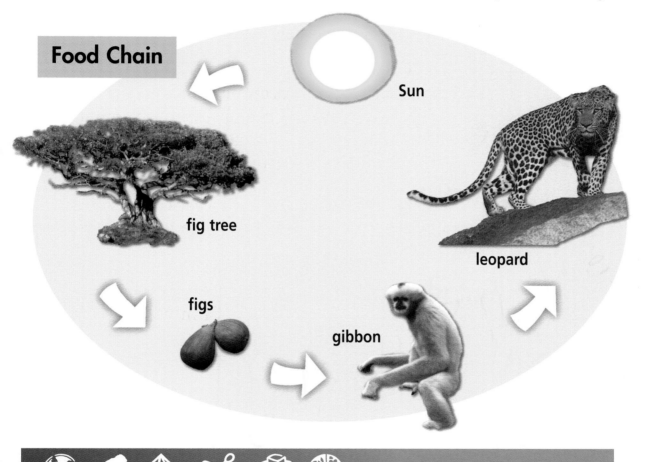

## Food Chain

Sun

fig tree

leopard

figs

gibbon

## Puzzler

Why does a marmoset monkey eat more than one type of food?

Answer: Eating many types of food helps an animal survive, especially when one type of food cannot be found. A marmoset can live on tree sap, tree gum, and insects when it cannot find fruit. These foods keep the marmoset healthy until new fruit grows in its territory.

# Primates of the Past

**P**rimates have been living on Earth for a long time. They have been around much longer than other mammals, such as dogs and horses. We know about ancient primates by the bones and other **fossils** they left behind.

Until about 65 million years ago, dinosaurs roamed Earth — and primates lived with them! At that time, most primates were very small. They searched for food at night, while many of the larger creatures were asleep.

*Plesiadapis* was a primate about the size of a squirrel. It lived during the time of the dinosaurs.

*Notharctus* lived in North America about 48 million years ago. It looked like a lemur and was one of the first primates to have a large brain.

Ancient lemurs lived in many areas of the world. Today, most lemurs live on the island of Madagascar.

## *Activity*

### Fossil Hunt

Visit a museum of natural history with a parent or a teacher. Look at fossils of animals. Try to imagine what each animal looked like and how it moved.

Ancient primates looked different from today's primates. Modern-day lemurs are the size of a cat or a small dog. Many years ago, however, some lemurs were as large as today's gorillas!

Although nonhuman primates live only in certain parts of the world today, they lived all over Earth in the past. Even North America was home to many types of primates.

# Monkey Business

**W**e know a lot about primates. A person who studies living primates is called a **primatologist**. Many primatologists study monkeys, apes, and lemurs in the wild. Other primatologists work with primates that live in zoos or research centers.

Primatologists spend a lot of time watching primates. They record what each troop member does and how it behaves. Careful study helps them learn how primates relate to each other.

**Some primatologists live near the primates they study.**

People who study primates that lived a long time ago are called **paleontologists**. These scientists dig for primate fossils. Fossils help them learn about the types of primates that no longer exist.

Many primatologists and paleontologists teach in universities to share with students what they know about primates.

## Activity

### Do Your Own Research

Ask a parent or a teacher to help you learn about these interesting careers:

- biologist
- environmentalist
- paleontologist
- primatologist
- wildlife photographer
- zookeeper

Paleontologists travel all over the world looking for fossils of animals and plants that are no longer living.

Primatology students learn how certain primates behave around other primates, including humans.

# Primates in Danger

Half of the nonhuman primates alive today are **endangered**. Some people hunt primates, such as gorillas, even though hunting them is against the law. Other people steal baby chimpanzees and monkeys from their habitats to sell as pets. A baby chimpanzee might seem like a nice pet until it grows into a large, strong animal!

Some humans cut down rain forests where many primates live. They want to clear the land to plant crops and raise cattle. Clearing forests destroys the homes of primates and many other creatures. To save endangered primates, people must protect the rain forests.

Some people capture wild primates to sell. Selling wild primates is illegal.

**How can people help endangered primates? Here are a few things you can do:**

1. Help save the rain forests. Think of ways humans and animals can live together in rain forest areas. Ask your teacher to make the study of rain forest animals a class project.
2. Do not buy a monkey for a pet. It is illegal to buy or sell wild primates.
3. Write to a primate conservation group to learn more about endangered primates. Many of these groups have information and activities for young people.

Some types of primates are almost extinct. You can help save them by preserving primate habitats, such as rain forests.

# Sounds and Signals

**M**ost primates can **communicate**. They let family members know what they are feeling and thinking by making sounds and movements. Some primates roar, while others hoot. A few make laughing sounds. Their sounds and signals tell other troop members what they want. Primates also use sounds to warn others about danger.

Howler monkeys have 15 to 20 different calls. They also make faces to communicate how they feel.

Some chimpanzees and gorillas are able to communicate with humans. These apes live in research centers, where they have learned sign language to express what they want to eat or what they want to do. They can even sign what their favorite color is!

Nonhuman primates need help from a human to learn sign language, but they do not use sign language the same way humans do. For example, apes do not use long sentences. Instead, they use gestures to make short, simple statements.

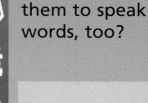

## Puzzler

Gorillas and chimpanzees can learn to use sign language. Is it possible for them to speak words, too?

Answer: Scientists have not been able to teach apes to speak. Their tongues and voices cannot make human sounds. Humans are the only primates that can make human sounds.

A female gorilla named Koko uses sign language to communicate with her trainer. Koko and her trainer have worked together for more than 25 years.

# Get the Message?

**H**umans and many other primates make faces. Their expressions show how they feel. How do you think these primates feel? Do you agree with the messages suggested?

I like you.

I am upset.

What other messages might these primates be trying to send? Compare their faces to the faces people make.

Stay away!

I am Tired.

## Glossary

**carnivores:** animals that eat mostly meat.

**communicate:** to pass on information.

**distinctive:** having a special quality or appearance.

**endangered:** dying out as a unique group of animals or plants.

**fossils:** the remains of animals or plants found hardened in layers of rock.

**frugivores:** animals that eat mostly fruit.

**juvenile:** no longer a baby but not yet an adult.

**mammal:** an animal that has fur or hair and produces live young that feed on their mother's milk.

**marsupials:** mammals whose babies grow inside their mother's pouch until they are old enough to walk.

**omnivores:** animals that eat both plants and animals.

**paleontologists:** scientists who study fossils of plant and animal groups that no longer exist.

**predators:** animals that hunt and eat other animals.

**primatologist:** a scientist who studies living primates.

**three-dimensional vision:** the ability to see the height, width, and depth of an object.

## Index

## Web Sites

www.EnchantedLearning.com/subjects/apes

www.janegoodall.org

www.koko.org

www.selu.com/bio/PrimateGallery

Some web sites stay current longer than others. For further web sites, use your search engines to locate the following topics: *ape, chimpanzee, monkey, primate, primatologist,* and *zoo.*